Fire in the
Sky

Fire in the Sky

by Candice F. Ransom
illustrations by Shelly O. Haas

Carolrhoda Books, Inc. / Minneapolis

To Taylor—C.F.R.

To my father, who was strengthened by both the larger-than-life events and the marbles of his childhood—S.O.H.

Special thanks to Micah and Jimmy—S.O.H.

Text copyright © 1997 by Candice F. Ransom
Illustrations copyright © 1997 by Shelly O. Haas

Library of Congress Cataloging-in-Publication Data

Ransom, Candice F.
    Fire in the sky / by Candice F. Ransom ; illustrations by Shelly O. Haas.
       p. cm.
    Summary: More than losing at marbles, worrying about his relatives in
 Germany, or hearing his favorite radio hero, Jack Armstrong, nine-year-old
 Stenny Green is focused on getting to see the Hindenburg when it lands near
 his home in Lakehurst, New Jersey, in 1937.
    ISBN 0-87614-867-4
    1. Hindenburg (Airship)—Juvenile fiction. [1. Hindenberg (Airship)—
 Fiction. 2. Family life—Fiction.] I. Haas, Shelly O., ill. II. Title.
 PZ7.R1743Fi 1997
 [Fic]—dc20   96-5739

Manufactured in the United States of America
1 2 3 4 5 6 – JR – 02 01 00 99 98 97

Contents

Chapter One

The Marble Chump

Stenny Green was losing. He wasn't surprised. He always lost at everything.

Click-clack.

"Got another one!" Buzzie Martinelli crowed. He scooped up Stenny's favorite moonstone marble and put it with the growing pile. Then he leaned down, aimed, and shot again.

Stenny shifted his weight. It was uncomfortable kneeling in his school pants. The waist was pretty tight, even though his mother had moved the button over twice. Maybe he shouldn't have eaten two hot dogs for lunch. Stenny's mother always fed him a big meal when he went home for the midday break.

"You awake, *Sten*wood?" Buzzie teased. He knew that Stenny hated his full name. But at least Buzzie hadn't called him Chubbo, the way he sometimes did in class. "Say good-bye to that blue cat's-eye."

"It's not a very good marble." Stenny tried to sound as though he didn't really care. But it looked like he would never even get a turn, much less win the game. He wondered what Jack Armstrong, the hero of his favorite radio program, would do if he were here. Jack Armstrong wouldn't let Buzzie Martinelli win. Stenny pushed his glasses up on his nose. He wondered if the Jack Armstrong Hovering Disc he had sent away for had come in the mail that day.

"Missed!" Buzzie said suddenly.

Stenny stared at the circle drawn in the dirt. Incredibly, a stray pebble had caused Buzzie's marble to skitter past the target.

"My turn," Stenny said.

Now was his chance! He hunkered down, aiming his best shooter carefully at one of Buzzie's marbles. Nervously, he pushed his straight blond hair off his damp forehead and shot. The large yellow-striped marble rolled feebly across the bumpy ground, stopping two inches short of Buzzie's marble.

"You missed," Buzzie said cheerfully. Then he proceeded to win the rest of Stenny's marbles.

When it was over, Buzzie stuffed Stenny's marbles into a bulging marble sack along with his own. He never played for anything but keeps. "Good game," he said.

Stenny's own marble sack was pathetically empty. "It wasn't a fair game," he protested.

"What do you mean?"

"It's too hot today," Stenny complained. It *was* unseasonably hot for the fifth of May. "New Jersey is never this hot this early."

Buzzie burst out laughing. "Stenny Green, you just kill me! Anyway, I'm still the marble champ."

"Marbles are dumb," Stenny said. "I have more important things on my mind."

"Like what? That zero on your arithmetic test?"

Stenny winced. Fourth grade arithmetic was too hard. He would rather read any day. Or work on his model of the *Hindenburg,* the famous airship. "I was busy thinking about tomorrow," he said, "when the *Hindenburg* gets here. This is its first flight of 1937."

Buzzie shrugged. "So tell me something new." Of course Buzzie knew when the dirigible was arriving. Buzzie's father was a member of the civilian ground crew. When the steam whistle blew, men all over town left their jobs or their homes and hurried to the nearby Naval Air Station. Many hands were needed to help land the huge airship, which traveled from Frankfurt, Germany, to Stenny's hometown of Lakehurst, New Jersey.

"I've seen the *Hindenburg* a zillion times," Buzzie patted back a yawn.

"No, you haven't," Stenny corrected. "It only made ten flights here last year."

"Same thing," Buzzie said.

"Have you ever been *on* the *Hindenburg?*" Stenny asked, knowing the answer. "I'm going on it tomorrow. My brother is getting me a special pass." Well, he *might* tour the *Hindenburg.* He hadn't obtained permission yet. But Buzzie didn't know that.

Buzzie looked at Stenny skeptically. "You said that last year. And you never got on it."

"Well, last year Michael was busy."

Stenny's nineteen-year-old brother was an enlisted man at the Naval Air Station. He was studying to become an airship navigator at the Naval Aerological School. He would help guide an airship by planning and charting its course.

Buzzie scooped his bike off the lawn. "See you in school tomorrow."

"I may be late!" Stenny called after him. "I don't know how long that tour will take. Maybe three or four hours!"

"Yeah, sure!" Buzzie raced down Cedar Street.

Stenny went inside his house. His mother was fixing supper. Pot roast, from the smell of it. An apple pie cooled on the windowsill.

"Hi, Ma," Stenny said. "Did I get anything in the mail today?"

"Not today." Mrs. Green frowned. "How many times have I told you not to play in your good clothes?"

"I'll change."

In his room, Stenny changed into play clothes. Lately they didn't fit very well, either. But his only other clothes were for temple.

Stenny went over to his bureau and picked up the model he was building. It wasn't easy making a replica of the *Hindenburg,* but Stenny wanted to get it just right.

"The *Hindenburg* is a dirigible," he said, liking the sound of his own voice. "Sometimes a dirigible is called an airship. It is not a balloon, even though it looks like one. Dirigibles are engine driven. You can steer them. The *Hindenburg* is a zeppelin, an airship with a rigid body, invented by a German man, Count von Zeppelin."

Stenny touched the tiny balsa wood box attached to the bottom of his model. That was the control car, where the officers flew the airship. The framework of the real *Hindenburg* was made of duralumin girders, strong but lightweight. The outside skin was fashioned from heavy cotton fabric, waterproofed and painted silver.

Stenny's model was ten inches long, not 803 feet. He had made it out of scraps of aluminum from his father's hardware store. The frame was covered with fabric from an old sheet. When his model was finished, Stenny would hang it from fishing line over his bed, where he could see it first thing in the morning and last thing at night.

The real *Hindenburg* had big pockets inside filled with hydrogen, a gas that was lighter than air. Stenny wished he could make his model fly, but his father said hydrogen was dangerous—so forget that idea.

Now Stenny frowned. Something about the model wasn't right. He had overlooked some important detail. He ought to go through his scrapbook and see what was missing.

The clock on Stenny's night table told him it was almost 5:15. His favorite program was on. Stenny ran into the living room and switched on the Philco. Then he settled himself on the blue rug in front of the radio. The announcer cried, "The All-American Boy!" as a chorus swelled into the "Hudson High Fight Song."

Then came the Wheaties commercial. Stenny hugged his knees. He ate Wheaties cereal every single day, just like Jack Armstrong. He saved the box tops and sent away for premiums. He already had a Whistle Ring. If only his Hovering Disc had come today. He imagined using the disc to save Jack Armstrong if Jack got in trouble. Not that Jack Armstrong needed saving. He was the best! He could fly a plane and sail a ship. Jack Armstrong could do anything.

"Stenny!" his mother called. "Come set the table."

"When my show is over," he called back.

"Now, please."

Sighing, Stenny turned the radio up louder so he could hear it. In the kitchen, he took plates from the cupboard.

"Four places," his mother remarked. "Remember, your brother is coming for dinner tonight."

"I didn't forget."

How could he forget? His brother ate dinner with them every Wednesday. Michael would sit across from Stenny, tall and thin in his dazzling white uniform, and talk about his exciting life at the air station.

Music trumpeted from the radio. Stenny's program was over. Oh, well. He'd listen to Jack Armstrong tomorrow. Picturing the radio character, Stenny saw his brother's strong chin, his flinty gray eyes. Stenny wanted to be just like Jack Armstrong. He wanted to lead safaris in Africa and expeditions to the North Pole. Most of all, he longed to pilot his own airship. That would be better than being an airship navigator any day.

Then he remembered playing marbles with Buzzie Martinelli. Stenny couldn't even win a simple game, much less fly an airship on great adventures. Instead of being the marble champ, Stenny Green was just a marble *chump*.

Chapter Two

Stenny's Zeppelin

Stenny's brother was late for dinner. Mrs. Green glanced worriedly at the phone. "He usually calls. It's not like him to be late, especially since we see so little of him. And I made pot roast."

"He's always here for Wednesday supper. And you always make his favorite food," Stenny said, trying to keep jealousy from his voice.

"Let's hold dinner," Mr. Green suggested. "A few minutes won't hurt."

It would hurt Stenny. He was starving. Then he wondered if his brother's tardiness had something to do with the *Hindenburg*. "Isn't the *Hindenburg* supposed to land this evening?" he asked. "I didn't hear the whistle."

Mr. Green shook his head. "The last I heard, it's not due until early tomorrow sometime." Just then the door banged open and Michael strode into the dining room. His normally spotless seaman's uniform was filthy, and his face was streaked with soot.

"Michael!" Mrs. Green cried. "What happened?"

"It's nothing, Ma."

"Nothing! Stenny, get your brother a glass of water."

"I can't stay," Michael said apologetically. "Sorry I didn't call, but we've been busy today."

Mr. Green looked at Michael solemnly. "Is it the fire?" he asked.

"Yeah. They're even evacuating people around Toms River. The guys from Fort Dix have been on the scene since lunchtime. Thanks, kid." Michael gratefully accepted the glass of water Stenny handed him.

"What fire?" Stenny asked.

Michael explained that the piney woods northwest of the Naval Air Station were on fire. Now smoke blew over the airfield, jeopardizing the *Hindenburg*'s landing. Local fire departments and the navy landing crew couldn't battle the blaze alone, so troops from nearby Fort Dix had been called in to help.

"Jack Armstrong wouldn't call in the army," Stenny said, pretending to wield a heavy fire hose. "He'd put that fire out all by himself."

Michael laughed. "I don't doubt it!"

"Can't you stay and eat?" Mrs. Green asked him.

"It's pot roast and apple pie," Stenny added. Maybe his brother would take him to see the fire after supper.

Michael grinned. "You can have my slice of pie, Sten. I have to get back to the base."

"Just be careful," Mr. Green warned.

"Can I go, too?" Stenny asked.

"Of course not!" his mother said.

Stenny considered jumping on his bike after supper and racing off to see the fire anyway. But in truth, he was afraid of fires. Even barbecue pits made him nervous. Buzzie Martinelli would laugh like crazy if he knew.

Michael headed toward the door. "I wish I could stay, folks, but the *Hindenburg* is coming in early tomorrow morning and the CO is already antsy about this fire."

"Michael?" Stenny asked hopefully, following him to the door. "Do you think your commanding officer—er, CO—would let me see the *Hindenburg*?"

"Not this time, Sten."

Stenny's face fell. "Phooey. I'll never get a tour."

"Since this is the *Hindenburg*'s first flight of the year, security is kind of tight. Because of the way things are in Germany lately, people are afraid something might happen to the airship," Michael told them.

Mr. Green nodded. "Hitler."

Stenny had seen Adolf Hitler in newsreels. With his toothbrush mustache and silly hairstyle, Germany's leader looked like a cartoon character. He was always ranting and shaking his fist. Hitler's troops, the black-booted Nazis, filled Stenny with a thrilling fear. Hitler was the kind of enemy Jack Armstrong would fight, Stenny thought. But first Jack would have to beat up all the other Nazis—

"Germany is preparing for war," Mr. Green said solemnly, interrupting Stenny's daydream. "I'm a little surprised the *Hindenburg* is coming at all."

"The Zeppelin Company has an agreement with our navy," Michael said. "That's why the Hindenburg is allowed to land here. They don't want war."

"Don't you think our government might be a little nervous?" Mr. Green said. "Zeppelins were used during the Great War to drop bombs on London. They could be used for war again."

Stenny had read about the raids by an early zeppelin pilot, Captain Ernst Lehmann. As a young naval officer, Captain Lehmann had piloted a passenger airship in Germany. When war broke out in Europe in 1914, Lehmann had fearlessly flown his zeppelin on bombing runs over the English Channel.

"The *Hindenburg* is a passenger airship," Michael pointed out. "It's only used for peacetime purposes."

"Situations change," Mr. Green argued.

Michael put on his white seaman's cap. "Well, I need to get back to the base before my CO declares war on me."

Stenny walked outside with him. "Are you sure I can't get on the *Hindenburg?*" he asked. For the *Hindenburg*'s first flight last year, a hundred thousand sightseers had come to marvel at the new wonder. Tourists had been allowed to go inside the hangar where the airship was stored, but not to board the airship itself.

Stenny's brother ruffled his hair. "Maybe on its next trip, when things aren't so hectic."

"Will you tell your CO that I'm an expert? I know everything there is to know about the *Hindenburg,*" Stenny added persuasively.

"You'll be first on the list." Michael got into his jalopy and drove down Cedar Street. Stenny hopped on his bike and pedaled after him. For a while he was able to keep pace. But at the corner the car picked up speed and Stenny fell behind. He gave up the chase, panting. Even a dog moved faster than he did. Jack Armstrong could outrun a car, easy, he thought.

Stenny could smell the smoke from the fire. The early evening sky was hazy with gray wisps. Even the thought of fire raging through the woods sent shivers down his spine. Stenny turned his bike around and slowly walked back home.

His parents were in the living room, listening to Lowell Thomas intone the news. Stenny got out his *Hindenburg* scrapbook and settled onto the carpet in front of the radio.

He *did* know everything there was to know about the zeppelin. Ever since the huge dirigible had made its maiden voyage last year, Stenny had cut out every newspaper and magazine article about it and pasted the articles into a scrapbook.

The *Hindenburg* was nearly one-sixth of a mile long from the bow, or front, to the stern, or rear. It could travel eighty miles an hour. Inside the belly of the ship were two decks containing heated passenger quarters and public rooms. The dining room was big enough to seat fifty passengers, with fine linens and real silverware. An aluminum piano, covered in yellow pigskin, had been

specially built for the airship. The *Hindenburg* was the last word in luxury travel.

Stenny's mother spoke during a break in the broadcast. "I had a letter from my sister in Germany today. She said that Jews have to sit on certain benches now. Grocery stores have signs that say Jews Not Admitted."

Mr. Green rustled his newspaper. "More of Hitler's doing. Where will that man stop?"

"Who knows?" Mrs. Green said. "But I worry about my sister and her family. Over there with that madman." Stenny's mother talked about Hitler as if the German leader were a crazy neighbor.

On top of the radio was a photograph in a silver frame—Stenny's German relatives. His Aunt Gerda and Uncle Frederick lived in Berlin. Stenny had a cousin, Franz, whom he had never met. He and Franz were the same age, nine. His mother often urged him to write to his German cousin. But Stenny wasn't really interested. Besides, he had more immediate worries.

He wondered if he could be sick tomorrow, so he could stay home from school. That way, the others would think he was touring the airship. As he listened to the serial *Mr. Keen, Tracer of Lost Persons,* he glanced over at the photograph again. In the warm May evening Stenny shivered, but he didn't know why.

Chapter Three

No Kind
of Hero

The next morning, Stenny lingered in bed. When his mother came in for the third time, he told her he didn't feel well. Mrs. Green felt his forehead. "You don't feel hot. Does your stomach hurt?"

"Yes," Stenny said. Then he realized his mother might give him a dose of cod-liver oil. "No," he said quickly. "I mean, everything kind of hurts."

After taking his temperature, Stenny's mother pronounced him well enough to go to school. Stenny reluctantly got dressed. Whenever he *needed* to stay home sick, it never worked. Now all the kids would know he wasn't taking a tour of the *Hindenburg.*

"Did the *Hindenburg* land?" Stenny asked over his

morning bowl of Wheaties. He knew the airship always docked at six in the morning or six in the evening. This way, the people in the civilian landing crew weren't called away from their regular jobs at all hours.

"It's late," his mother replied. "Now it's supposed to come in tonight."

Stenny's heart leaped with hope. It was safe to go to school! Nobody would expect him to be touring an airship that hadn't arrived yet. "Why is it late?" he wondered aloud.

"Something about strong head winds, bad weather over the Atlantic." His mother poured him a glass of juice. "It rained last night and put out that fire, thank heavens." Stenny was glad about that, too. Now the *Hindenburg* could land safely.

When he finished his breakfast, Stenny gathered up his schoolbooks and rode his bike to school. Buzzie Martinelli was standing by the bike rack. As usual, other boys from their class were gathered around him. "Hey, Stenwood," Buzzie said. "The *Hindenburg* is late. What about your tour?"

Buzzie had offered him a perfect excuse. Stenny could say he couldn't take the tour because the *Hindenburg* was late. Then Stenny saw Buzzie's fat marble sack dangling from his belt. He bet Buzzie had told all the kids how he had beat Stenny at marbles yesterday.

"I'm still going," Stenny heard himself say. "I'm just going tonight instead of this morning."

Frank Grafius's eyes narrowed with disbelief. "Says who, the king of England? You're going on a tour every time the *Hindenburg* comes in."

"I'm telling the truth," Stenny said.

"Prove it," demanded Bill Little.

"Yeah, prove it," Buzzie echoed. "Let's see your pass."

"My brother has it," Stenny said quickly. A few seconds ago he felt safe. Now he was caught in his fib again.

"If Michael can get you a pass, he can get one for me," Buzzie said. "I want to go, too."

Stenny took off his glasses and polished the lenses on his shirt. "The invitation is only for me," he said nervously.

"Get one for me, too. You're always bragging about the pull you have at the air station."

"I really don't think—" Stenny began.

"I'll give you back all the marbles I won from you," Buzzie offered. "I'll even give you my lucky shooter." A stunned silence followed this statement. Buzzie Martinelli was the undisputed marble champion of the fourth grade. His peppermint-swirled shooter was famous. No one in his right mind would turn him down.

Stenny drew in a breath. He couldn't get Buzzie an invitation. He didn't have one himself. Now he would have to admit he had made up the whole tour business. That was worse than losing to Buzzie Martinelli.

Just then the bell rang. The students rushed through the front door. In his classroom, Stenny sank into his seat, grateful he wouldn't have to say anything more about the tour for a while.

After the flag salute and roll call, the class began their history lesson. Mrs. Hoffmyer's fourth graders were working on reports. Stenny had chosen to do his report on George Washington. He had heard a story about how young George Washington had chopped down a cherry tree. When George's father demanded to know who had cut down the tree, George had answered, "I cannot tell a lie. I did it."

Heavyhearted, Stenny doodled zeppelins in his notebook. Even as a little boy, George Washington had been brave. He had gone on to be the father of his country. Somehow courage seemed to come easy to everyone but Stenny.

When the last bell of the day rang, Stenny was the first out the door. He grabbed his bike from the rack. He wanted to get away before Buzzie or any of the others could ask about going on the tour. But he couldn't outride Buzzie Martinelli.

"Stenny! Wait up!" Buzzie called. He easily caught up with Stenny.

At the drugstore on the corner, Stenny stopped and parked his bike. Maybe he could ditch Buzzie here. "I want to go in here a minute," he said.

They stepped into the cool gloom of the drugstore. Stenny checked the wooden rack of newspapers and magazines, hoping some new funny books had come in. The store radio was tuned to the baseball game. The Brooklyn Dodgers were playing the Pittsburgh Pirates this afternoon.

"I wonder who's winning," Buzzie said. He was a Dodgers fan.

The sportscaster broke off his description of the game to announce that the *Hindenburg* was sailing over Ebbets Field. The spectators and both teams were gazing at the magnificent sight.

"The *Hindenburg* is in New York," Stenny said. "It'll be here soon."

"And you'll get to go on it." Buzzie turned to Stenny with appealing eyes. "Ask your brother if I can come, too. *Please.*"

Stenny was amazed that brave Buzzie Martinelli, marble champ and fearless bike rider, was suddenly begging *him.* "I'll ask," he replied weakly.

Uncomfortable with his fibs, Stenny left the drugstore.

A real hero didn't make up stories, he thought morosely. But then, he wasn't any kind of hero.

Dinner in Stenny's house was served at five-thirty on the dot. Mr. Green wanted to be through eating by the time the news came on. Stenny could barely eat. It had rained twice since he had gotten home from school—drenching downpours. The sky threatened more rain. "Stenny, is your stomach still bothering you?" his mother wanted to know.

"I'm just not very hungry." He put down his fork. "May I be excused? I want to go out and play."

"Be home early," his mother said. "It's a school night."

"And don't go near the air station," Stenny's father

cautioned. "You know the rules." Stenny replied with a nod. He knew the rules. Spectators only got in the way when the airship was landing. Michael had complained often enough.

Outside, Stenny picked up his bike from the driveway. The sky was ominously black. Lightning darted through the swollen clouds. He glanced back at the house. By now, his parents would be settling in front of the radio to listen to the news. Stenny knew that if his mother got a look at the sky, she'd make him go in. But the Naval Air Station drew him like a magnet. He *had* to go see the *Hindenburg* land, even if it meant getting in trouble. He pointed his bike toward the landing field and pedaled as hard as he could.

When Stenny was halfway down the road, the skies opened. It was as if someone had overturned a washtub. Soaked, Stenny struggled to keep his bike off the muddy shoulder. He thought about turning around and going home. Jack Armstrong wouldn't be put off by a little rain, Stenny told himself, and kept pedaling.

It had stopped raining by the time he reached the main gate of the Naval Air Station. He hadn't heard the whistle calling the ground crew to their stations. And the airship wasn't looming over the field. He wasn't too late to see it land after all. Stenny straddled his bike. In front of him was a large sign that read:

ON ACCOUNT OF BRIEF STAY
AIRSHIP HINDENBURG
AT THIS PORT
THE PUBLIC CANNOT BE PERMITTED
AT THE MOORING LOCATION
OR ABOARD SHIP.

The sign didn't bother him. The very air seemed charged with electric excitement. The *Hindenburg* was on its way.

Chapter Four

Fire in the Sky

Stenny turned away from the sign. Cars were parked along the roadway, filled with people who had come to see the airship land or to pick up passengers. It was very humid. Stenny felt as if he were breathing through a wet washrag. He watched a woman who was towing three children hurry to her car. They were all soaked from the downpour. Once the four wet people were inside the car, the windows immediately steamed up.

Leaving his bike on the side of the muddy road, Stenny walked to the front gate. He wondered how he would get inside. The guard at the gate was busy talking to some people. Stenny sidled up to the edge of the group. There were two men and a woman, and two teenaged girls. Stenny hoped that no one would notice a nine-year-old boy.

"When is the airship going to land?" one of the men asked the guard, identifying himself as a reporter.

"I can't answer that, sir," the guard replied. "The men have been called to their stations twice. Twice the landing has been delayed."

"Can we go inside before it pours again?" the woman wanted to know. She seemed impatient. The guard busily checked papers, then nodded. The woman and the two men passed through the gate, heading for a shed at the edge of the landing field. Stenny knew that the shed was where reporters and radio newspeople waited. The landing of the *Hindenburg* was always an important event.

The girls moved up. Stenny stood a little behind them, his fingers crossed. "May I help you?" the guard inquired.

One of the girls told him they had driven down from Northfield to meet a couple of crew members. She named Franz Herzog, a navigator, and Franz Eichelmann, a radio operator. Stenny thought about his German cousin. A lot of boys in Germany were named Franz, it seemed.

The guard shook his head. "I'm sorry, ladies. But I can't—"

The other girl spoke up quickly. They had wired the *Hindenburg* earlier and they really *needed* to get inside the gate. It began to rain again. Not a downpour as before, but a light drizzle. The guard waved the girls through.

He never noticed Stenny slipping past. Once through the gate, Stenny followed the girls toward the shed.

Suddenly a steam whistle blew. Men streamed out of the hangar and from beneath the mooring mast, where they had taken shelter from the passing squalls. The mooring mast was a 75-foot-high structure that would hold the *Hindenburg* in place when it arrived. The seamen's white shirts were pasted to their backs with rain. Some of the civilians grumbled about getting wet all over again. Stenny ran excitedly to the shed. The airship was about to land!

Reporters and photographers were clustered inside the open doorway of the shed. A radio commentator gave instructions to his soundman. On the field, newsreelmen squatted on top of their cars, ready to film the event. Stenny edged behind the reporters. No one paid any attention to him. Several people were busy scribbling in their notebooks. The man next to Stenny muttered, "I hope this is it this time."

"The airship passed over the field," said another. "They should have landed then and gotten it over with."

The first man shook his head. "Not in this weather. They can't afford to take chances."

Stenny peered out across the sandy landing field to mooring circle number one. It was such a thrilling sight. The mooring mast had been pulled by tractor to a spot inside the circle, a couple of hundred feet from the hangar. A green light blinked atop the hanger roof. The light flashed the letter *L* in Morse code. Radio operators aboard the airship were in constant contact with the station. Once the operators were close enough to see the blinking light, they would reel in the airship's antennae.

The ground crew was in position. Aiding the 92 navy men stationed at the base, an additional crew of nearly 140 civilians swelled the ranks, although all were not needed on every landing. Buzzie's father was one of the civilian line handlers. A line handler's job was to grab one of the cables, or lines, dropped from the dirigible and to help pull in the airship and position it next to the mooring mast. Stenny's brother was a line handler, too. One day he would navigate airships, not dock them.

"My brother's out there!" Stenny said proudly.

"Which one is he?" asked one of the reporters.

Stenny squinted at the men assembled in two rows along the mooring field. From where he stood, all the uniformed men looked alike. "I can't really tell from here," he said. "But he's in the forward landing lines group."

The reporter nodded. "It takes a lot of men to haul in that monster."

Stenny knew exactly. "Sixty-eight men handle the forward lines. And another forty-six to handle the stern lines."

The man stared at him, clearly impressed. "How do you know so much?"

"I just do."

Bringing down an airship as big as the *Hindenburg* was a complicated procedure. When Stenny had first watched the airship land a year ago, from behind the fence, he'd thought it would land on the ground, like an airplane. But the ship remained in the air, hovering just above the ground, and the nose of the floating zeppelin was attached to the towerlike mooring mast. Two men stood at the top of the mooring mast. Their job was to grab the steel cable as it was wound out of the ship's nose and

connect the cable to the mast. Then the airship was reeled in.

The lower tail fin, at the rear of the airship, was then attached to a tail-lock car. This wheeled car sat on a railroad track that circled the mast. The car could roll along the track, supporting the end of the *Hindenburg* as it shifted in the wind. A set of rolling stairs pushed up to the passenger deck allowed the passengers to descend.

"It's coming!" someone cried. Reporters surged onto the field. Newsreelmen trained their cameras on the horizon and began cranking.

From the west, the magnificent zeppelin sailed into view, nosing through the twilight. Crossing the south fence, the ship moved in a graceful arc, until it hovered over the landing field. The spectators were silent. Everyone was in awe of the enormous airship, sailing overhead like a stately silver cloud. An arrow of sunlight struck the control car window, a ray of gold among the silver.

Stenny's heart lifted with joy. Was there ever a sight to match this? More than anything, he wanted to fly a dirigible. Piloting a zeppelin must be the most exhilarating feeling in the world.

The airship drifted forward and down. Stenny heard the huge propellers back up. The ship turned again, and a shower of water pelted from the stern tanks. Stenny knew that the water acted as ballast, a weight that helped control the movement of the dirigible. The captain was dumping ballast to level the ship.

A radio commentator began recording. "Here it comes, ladies and gentlemen, and what a sight it is, a thrilling one, a marvelous sight. It is coming down out of the sky pointed toward us, and toward the mooring mast. The mighty diesel motors roar, the propellers biting into the air. No one wonders that this great floating palace can travel through the air at such a speed with these powerful motors behind it."

Stenny didn't think the *Hindenburg* looked like a palace. It was more like a giant fish, a silvery whale plowing majestically through an ocean in the sky.

Lines began to drop from the nose of the airship. The idling engines were shut down. First, the starboard lines, the ones on the right, coiled onto the sand beneath the mooring mast. The port, or left, lines fell next. Navy men scuttled to grab the lines. They worked quickly to secure the airship.

Stenny noticed the newsreelmen pointing their cameras at the ground crew. The wind suddenly rose, smacking the airship broadside. The line handlers dug their heels into the wet sand. Unpredictable winds often made it difficult to tether the great ship.

Stenny had never seen the *Hindenburg* so close. He had always observed it from beyond the fence. He stared at the ship, memorizing its graceful lines. His glance lingered on the tail fins. Suddenly he knew what detail was missing from his model airship. Painted on both the upper and lower tail fins was a crooked cross called a swastika. The cross represented Hitler's new government, the Third Reich. The *Hindenburg* was flying the flag of Nazi Germany.

A chill rippled down Stenny's backbone. Why had he never seen the swastika on all the photographs of the *Hindenburg?* The flag had always been there. He had simply never noticed it until now.

He noticed something else, a strange orange glow just forward of the upper fin. The pinkish orange glow brightened, lighting the interior of the ship like a Japanese lantern. Stenny could see the intricate framework of girders clearly, as if the ship were an egg held up to a candle. Then, with a roaring *whoosh,* the glow exploded into a fireball that lit the sky.

Chapter Five

The End of the World

Flames quickly engulfed the airship. Stenny had never realized the rocket power of hydrogen until now. The pockets of gas inside the airship were feeding the fire at an alarming speed. Bits of burning linen parachuted to earth. Molten aluminum dripped like an ice-cream cone. It all happened so quickly no one had time to react. It was like the end of the world.

Someone near the mooring mast yelled, "Run for your lives!" The line handlers scattered as the huge airship listed downward, tail first.

The radio newsman sobbed hysterically into his microphone, "It's burst into flames! Get this, Charlie," he ordered his cameraman. "Get out of the way, please, oh my, this is terrible, oh my, get out of the way, please! It's burning, bursting into flames and is falling. . . . this is one of the worst catastrophes in the world! It's a terrific sight. . . . oh, the humanity and all the passengers!"

Now the spectators broke their stunned silence. People screamed as the *Hindenburg* plummeted toward the ground. They pushed out of the shed. Stenny's heart leaped into his throat. "Look!" he exclaimed to the reporter standing next to him.

An object smashed through one of the windows lining the passenger deck. Two men climbed out. A third followed. All three hung precariously from the airship. "They're going to jump!" Stenny cried.

"They'll never make it," the man said. "The ship must be more than a hundred feet in the air." One of the men, who was clinging to the jacket of another man, lost his grip. He dropped, arms flailing, onto the wet sand below. He landed spread-eagled and seemed to bounce as he hit the ground. The second man fell heavily onto the sand. The third man waited until the ship had sunk lower. Then he let go, curling his legs under him. As he hit the ground, he rolled. Stenny was astonished to see the man stand up and brush himself off. He limped away.

The landing field was pandemonium. The ground crew scurried from beneath the sinking fireball. Passengers and airship crewmen hurled themselves from the flaming zeppelin. Spectators shrieked in terror. Suddenly a voice on a bullhorn bellowed, "NAVY MEN! STAND FAST!" Stenny recognized that voice from his brother's description of Chief Boatswain Fred Tobin. The navy men and civilian line handlers reversed and began running back toward the burning airship. Reporters and spectators ran forward, too. Stenny was swept along with them. He didn't have time to be afraid.

The *Hindenburg* was listing sharply, like a deflating balloon. Wind fanned the fire toward the starboard side. Along the hull, the body of the ship, the letters that spelled out *Hindenburg* were gobbled one by one by hungry flames. The stern hit the ground beneath the mooring mast. The ship cracked in two with a second rocking explosion.

The explosion deafened Stenny. He could hear nothing for a second. Then he heard a high-pitched scream. He looked up. The windows on the port side were nearly level with the ground. Two little boys stood framed in a flaming window. A hand reached out and shoved them. A man below caught the first boy, throwing him out of the fiery path. The second boy fell at the man's feet. His hair was on fire. The man dragged the child away, beating at the flames. From the burning wreckage, a girl leaped. Her hair and back were on fire. Two men rushed forward and pulled her away from the ship.

Stenny could not breathe. The smoke and horrible sights paralyzed his chest. His eyes stung from the intense heat. He did not belong here. He wanted to go home. Unable to see for all the smoke, Stenny tripped over a line half-buried in the wet sand. As he staggered to one knee, he looked up to see a man and a woman walking arm in arm down the main gangway. They looked dazed. The man began to cry. Several men from the landing crew rushed up the ramp to assist them.

Many of the people who had survived the crash now risked their own lives to help others. A man in a charred business suit sobbed brokenly, "I couldn't save him! I couldn't save him!" Stenny didn't know who he referred to, but the man's anguish pierced his heart.

Cars screeched onto the landing field. Passengers and crew were being loaded into the vehicles, eyes glazed with shock, clothes burned to tatters. Many held their scorched hands in front of them. The victims reminded Stenny of broken dolls. The man in the business suit climbed into a car, still sobbing.

Stenny hesitated. Ahead he could see the cavelike hangar, a safe haven. If he went inside, he could get away from all the horror. Then he turned back toward the *Hindenburg*. Amazingly, people still crawled from the burning wreckage. Stenny wondered how anyone could survive such a fire. He could feel terror in the air. Everyone was afraid—they were no different from Stenny. Yet they went back into the flames again and again. Or they walked through fire to reach safety. He could not leave. He had to help those people.

Swallowing his own fears, Stenny ran back into the smoke.

Chapter Six

Thirty-four Seconds

Stenny bumped into a crumpled form. It was a man on his hands and knees. He was alive, frantically trying to burrow into the wet sand.

"You're okay!" Stenny told him. He steered the man toward the hangar.

The *Hindenburg* was reduced to girders and struts, outlined by flames. Steel cables and other trailing debris sizzled like white-hot snakes. Stenny tried to stay well away from the danger.

Just then a teenaged boy staggered blindly into Stenny's path. His hair and clothing were drenched. He was blank faced with confusion.

"This way," Stenny said, clutching the boy's sleeve.

The boy looked as if he had been dunked in the Atlantic. His clothing hissed with steam. Stenny thought of soggy mittens left to dry on radiator vents.

As Stenny turned toward the hangar, someone collided with him. The man gripped him by the shoulders to peer into his face. His uniform was soaked in patches and streaked with soot. His face was tense. "Stenny!" Michael exclaimed in astonishment. "What on earth are you doing here?"

"I—" Nothing but a croak emerged from Stenny's heat-seared throat.

His brother yanked him away from the fire. "Get out of here, Stenny, before you get hurt."

"Lots of people are already hurt," Stenny managed to say. "I'm helping with the rescue."

Just then, Michael noticed the teenaged boy swaying on unsteady legs. Stenny tightened his grasp on the boy's sleeve.

"It's okay," Stenny told his brother. "We're going to get help."

Michael's face relaxed a little. "You'll find medics in the hangar. Wait for me there, Sten." With a final clap on his brother's arm, Michael disappeared into the swirling smoke.

Stenny led the boy across the sand to the hangar. The boy said something. Stenny didn't understand German, but figured the boy might have thanked him. "You're welcome," he replied.

At the doorway of the hangar, Stenny turned to gawk at the flaming, twisted carcass that was once the mightiest airship to rule the skies. The great silvery form looked like a dying dragon. He had no idea how much time had passed since the first fireball. It seemed like hours. The landing field was a nightmare. The world outside the perimeter fence no longer existed. Then he heard the wail of sirens. Ambulances and fire equipment were rushing to the scene. The outside world was coming to them after all.

Inside the hangar Stenny met another nightmare. Passengers and crew members from the crashed airship were everywhere, coughing, sobbing, murmuring in German and English. Burn victims sprawled on tables and on the floor, moaning and screaming in their pain. Sailors bustled around with stretchers, carrying victims to the base infirmary.

Piled on tables and on the floor were heaps of fruit baskets, flowers, and cheerfully wrapped packages—gifts for the returning passengers. Stenny had forgotten that this was the *Hindenburg's* first flight of the season. Passengers had been eagerly expecting to end their long journey. All their hopes had exploded over the mooring circle.

Gently floating over the confusion was the American

airship *Los Angeles.* Stenny looked up at the dirigible, which was much smaller than the *Hindenburg,* and thought its helium-filled skin seemed to sag sadly.

A reporter shouted into a telephone. "We got it all on film!" he proclaimed. "Thirty-four seconds. That's the time from the second explosion till the ship crashed. I timed it."

The boy Stenny had escorted ran over to an officer in a scorched uniform. The man next to the officer wore only the brim of his hat. Tufts of charred hair stuck up from where the rest of his hat had been. The three began speaking rapidly in German.

The man in uniform came over to Stenny. In accented

English, he explained that the boy he had helped was Werner Franz, a cabin boy. A water tank had burst and emptied on him as he leaped through a flaming hatchway. The water saved his life. He was fourteen years old. Werner managed a lopsided grin. Stenny knew the grin said "Thanks."

Stenny went with Werner to the emergency dispensary being hastily set up on the field. As a doctor examined the German boy, Stenny saw the young man who had hung from the airship, fallen, and walked away. It turned out the man was an acrobat. He had broken his heel during his fall.

Werner Franz was pronounced fine. But many of the

other surviving passengers and crew members were not so lucky. Ambulances and private cars carted the wounded off to hospitals in nearby Lakewood and Asbury Park.

After Werner left with other crew members, Stenny went back to the hangar to look for Michael. He couldn't find him anywhere. Worrying that his brother might be injured, Stenny walked over to the base infirmary. Vehicles transporting the injured jounced past him. Thick, acrid-smelling smoke blanketed the area. Many newsreel cameras still rolled. The airship still burned furiously in the center of the field. The place looked worse than anything he had seen in a superhero movie serial.

No one stopped him at the door of the infirmary. The doctors and nurses were too busy treating the injured. The infirmary reeked of alcohol, disinfectant, and something else like burned meat. Stenny's stomach roiled. More than anything, he wanted to go home. But he couldn't leave until he had made sure his brother was not among the wounded.

A nurse tended to a man in blue coveralls that were burned to rags. "What are you doing here, son?" she demanded.

"I'm looking for my brother."

"Was he a passenger?" she asked. "He might be in the other room."

In the next room Stenny found a man and a woman, each sitting on opposite tables. The woman's coat was full of holes, and she wore only one shoe. She dabbed at her burned hands with a piece of gauze she kept dipping into a bottle of medicine. Across from her, the man stared with glazed blue eyes. His clothes were merely charred wisps. He had no hair left on his head. The woman passed the bottle over to him. The man didn't flinch as he quietly daubed his own burns. He didn't appear to be as bad off as some of the others. Something about the set of the man's shoulders and his calm, far-sighted gaze made Stenny stare at him. Neither of the patients noticed him.

A hand clamped on Stenny's shoulder. He jumped, startled. Then he nearly cried when he saw it was his brother.

"You shouldn't be here," Michael told him, pulling him from the room.

As they left, Stenny saw the man from the back. Then he quickly turned away. The man's injuries were far worse than Stenny had realized. The sight of shredded flesh would stay with him forever.

"Will that man die?" he asked Michael.

Michael hesitated.

"Do you know who he is?" Stenny demanded. "He's somebody important, isn't he?"

Michael's voice brimmed with respect and sadness. "I think it's Captain Lehmann."

Stenny gasped. Not Ernst Lehmann, the great zeppelin pilot? Stenny couldn't believe he'd actually been in the same room with him. The commander had never complained of his wounds, which must have been agonizing. A true hero.

"I hope he'll be all right," Stenny said. His brother did not reply.

Outside, Michael marched Stenny to the main gate. "I called Mom and Dad and let them know where you were. They wanted to drive over, but I told them you'd ride your bike home. It'd be faster."

Stenny saw why. Clamoring around the fence were hundreds of people. The police had cordoned off the area surrounding the field, but photographers, reporters, and curiosity seekers jostled each other at the fence, trying to glimpse the *Hindenburg*.

Michael elbowed his way through the throng, pushing Stenny in front of him. "Where's your bike?" he asked.

Stenny had left it at the gate. The road was jammed with cars, but he found his bike, still propped against a tree. "Go straight home," Michael ordered. "Mom and Dad are already frantic."

Stenny nodded. He had forgotten about his parents. They would have heard about the crash and realized

Stenny was missing. He cast one final glance over his shoulder. Beyond the teeming mob lay the smoldering hulk of the *Hindenburg*. If the reporter was right, the great airship had been completely destroyed in just thirty-four seconds.

Ordinary Hero

As Stenny pedaled down the road, he felt like a fish swimming upstream. Everyone in the world, it seemed, was heading toward the air station. He turned wearily down Cedar Street. By now it was dark. Stenny was tired, but the long evening wasn't over. He still had to face his parents.

His mother met him at the door. Her face was anxious as she folded Stenny in a smothering hug. "Are you okay?"

"I'm fine, Ma."

"We've been so worried." She gave him a loving shake. "Don't ever do that again! Your father is out looking for you."

Just then the family car pulled into the driveway. His

father climbed out. "It's madness over there," he declared. "You okay, Sten?"

"Yes, Pa. Didn't Michael tell you I'd ride my bike home?"

"Yes, he did. But I thought I'd see you on the road." His father sounded tired. "Missed you anyway."

Stenny felt bad he had put his parents through so much. "I'm sorry. I didn't mean to worry you."

His father sighed. "You had no idea there would be a disaster. No one did. Just so you're okay."

"I am. I'm just a little worn out."

"I'll make you some Ovaltine." Mrs. Green went into the kitchen. Left alone with his father, Stenny found himself staring at the floor.

"It was something, wasn't it?" his father said, as if he knew what Stenny had seen.

"It was terrible. The fire . . . all those people . . . " He couldn't finish. He remembered Captain Lehmann sitting on the infirmary table, calmly dabbing medicine on his burns. Stenny looked around at the familiar objects in the room—the radio and the blue carpet, his mother's mending abandoned in her chair. He realized how glad he was to be home.

All his life, he had craved grand adventure. Like Jack Armstrong, Stenny longed to guide safaris and pilot his own zeppelin around the world. But he had only imagined the exciting side of adventure. Tonight he had seen

the other side of adventure. People seriously injured, screaming in pain, stunned with shock. Some were dead. In movie serials and on radio programs, only the bad guys wound up dead.

Maybe heroes weren't dashing, fearless men like Jack Armstrong. Maybe they were ordinary people who pushed aside their own fears to help others. Sometimes they succeeded; sometimes they failed.

Stenny's mother returned with a glass of malted chocolate milk. Stenny drank gratefully. He was powerfully thirsty after breathing in so much smoke.

"I think you need to go to bed," said Mr. Green. "We'll talk more about this tomorrow."

After washing up, Stenny went into his room. His model of the *Hindenburg* sat on his desk, waiting for him to add the finishing touches. What was the point of completing it? he wondered as he pulled off his smoke-grimed clothes. The great zeppelin was gone.

Stenny climbed into bed and drew the covers up to his chin. His mother and father came in to say good night.

"Don't think about what happened tonight," his mother said, kissing his cheek. "Have sweet dreams." She picked up Stenny's dirty clothes on her way out.

"Good night, Sten," Mr. Green said.

"Dad," Stenny asked. "Am I going to be grounded?"

"Your mother and I have decided not to ground you this time," his father replied. "We don't think you'll go off without telling us again."

"Thanks, Dad. 'Night."

When his father left, Stenny rolled over. He had never been so tired. Behind his closed eyelids, he saw a bright flash. It was the *Hindenburg,* blowing up again. Stenny put the image out of his mind and finally drifted off to sleep.

The next morning, Stenny awoke to the loud shrieks of blue jays nesting in the pine tree next to his window. Stenny got up. Was he late for school? He put on his school clothes and went out to the kitchen. The radio blared news of last night's crash. He was surprised to see Michael sipping a cup of coffee. "What are you doing here?" he asked.

"Just came by to make sure you were okay." Dark circles ringed his brother's eyes.

"I'm fine," Stenny said. "Did you sleep at all?"

"Not much." Michael drained his cup. "I need to head back to the base. It's crazy over there." He paused. "I'm proud of you, Sten, for what you did last night." He thumped Stenny's shoulder, the way seamen greeted each other.

"It wasn't anything," Stenny mumbled. But his brother's touch made him feel ten feet tall.

When Michael left, Mrs. Green asked, "Do you feel like going to school today?"

"Yes, Ma."

As he ate his cereal, he listened to the broadcast. No one seemed to know what had caused the explosion. There were reports of St. Elmo's Fire, a glowing light caused by electricity in a thunderstorm. Stenny remembered the lightning-charged atmosphere. The casualty list was still growing. Some of the passengers and crewmen had died during the night. Stenny gathered his books and left the house.

Buzzie Martinelli was waiting on the corner. "Want to ride to school together?" he asked. Stenny was surprised. Buzzie usually dashed down the street like a stallion. The marble champ had never had time for Stenny before.

"I heard the crash," Buzzie remarked as they rode side by side. "It went KA-BOOM! My dad said it was something." Buzzie paused. "He said you were there."

Stenny nodded. He realized that many civilian line handlers, people he knew, had also witnessed the crash.

"How's your dad?" Stenny asked.

"He's okay. He's really tired, though." Buzzie pedaled in silence for a moment, then he said, "You didn't get your tour."

"Actually," Stenny admitted, "I was never invited on a tour. I made the whole thing up."

He thought Buzzie would jeer, but the other boy merely nodded, as if he understood. Then Buzzie asked, "Were you scared? I mean, when it blew up and all?"

"Yes," Stenny said. "I was."

At school Buzzie told the other kids that Stenny had witnessed the explosion. Suddenly Stenny was surrounded by people who wanted to talk about the disaster.

"What was it like?" Frank Grafius asked.

"I heard it was sabotage," Bill Little broke in. "A Nazi spy blew it up."

"Why would the Germans blow up their own airship?" Stenny said. "That doesn't make sense."

Bill shrugged. "It could have been an American spy.

Nobody likes what the Germans are doing these days."

Stenny remembered his aunt's letter saying that Jews were only allowed to sit on certain benches. The spidery swastika symbol flickered through his mind. The Nazis seemed more menacing now—they weren't just a group of bad guys on a movie serial.

Frank said, "What do you think happened to the *Hindenburg*, Stenny? You were *there.*"

"I don't know," Stenny replied. "It just . . . exploded."

The others stared at him in awe.

When the bell rang and they all went to their seats, the teacher asked Stenny if he wanted to talk about his adventure.

"Maybe tomorrow," Stenny muttered.

At lunchtime, Buzzie asked Stenny to play kickball with him and the guys. Stenny had never been so popular. Everyone acted like he was a big hero. But he didn't feel like a hero. He felt like an ordinary boy. He had seen the crash all right. But he had also seen the victims.

When school was out, Buzzie said to him, "Let's go out to the field and see what's going on."

Stenny had thought he never wanted to visit the air station again. But he realized the landing field was part of their lives. "Okay, but I have to ask my mom first." His mother gave permission but warned the boys to stay out of the way.

The road was still thronged with cars. Every news report seemed to bring more onlookers. At the fence the boys joined the crowd of spectators. Investigators pored over the rubble. No one else was permitted inside. A man showed them a charred scrap of fabric. "This is part of the hull. I got it before the guard threw everybody out. There's not much left."

Stenny grasped the fence, pressing his face against the metal wires. He stared at the skeleton of the *Hindenburg*. The only recognizable part left was a tail fin. The half-burned swastika pointed toward the clear blue sky. A mockingbird sang in the treetops. The grass and piney woods smelled fresh after yesterday's storm. It seemed hard to believe that a terrible tragedy had taken place.

The *Hindenburg* was gone forever. But the Third Reich, the people behind the swastika, still ruled Germany. An ominous power lurked in that stark, black cross. Something—Stenny didn't know what—was going to happen. They would have to face whatever lay in the future. And they would have to be brave. Even ordinary people, like him.

As Stenny turned away from the fence, he decided he would take his model to school tomorrow. He would tell the class all about the greatest airship in the world. Maybe his teacher would hang it in one corner of the classroom. That way, no one would ever forget the *Hindenburg*. Tonight, though, he would write to his cousin Franz in Germany. He had a lot to tell him.

Afterword

On its final flight, the *Hindenburg* carried ninety-seven people, sacks of mail, airplane parts, a lady's dress, two dogs, and three partridge eggs.

Thirty-six people died in the crash: one ground crewman, thirteen passengers, and twenty-two airship crewmen, including Captain Lehmann. The officer who piloted the airship this trip, Captain Pruss, survived. There were a total of sixty-two survivors.

The cause of the crash remains a mystery. Before the voyage, there were threats that the *Hindenburg* would be destroyed on American soil. But no bomb fragments were found in the wreckage. Other theories include St. Elmo's Fire, static electricity, or an electrical failure on board the ship. Wherever it came from, a spark was necessary to ignite the hydrogen inside the hull.

The disaster brought an abrupt end to the age of rigid dirigibles. The U.S. Navy's airship operations had a poor track record. The rigid dirigibles *Akron, Macon,* and the *Shenandoah* had all crashed, killing many people. After the *Hindenburg* incident, the Navy switched to blimps, nonrigid airships kept aloft by helium, a safer, nonflammable gas.

After the accident, the political situation in Europe continued to heat up. Hitler's troops invaded Poland on September 1, 1939. This act sparked World War II. Six million Jews in European countries were killed during the war.

Blimps played a small role in World War II. The U.S. Navy employed them to detect enemy submarines along both coasts of the United States.